Fic   Crofford, Emily
Cro
        A matter of pride

DATE DUE

MAY 25 '85		
tucker		
OCT 23 '86		
SEP 24 '87		
NOV 12 '87		
NOV 3 '88		
APR 23 '91		

A
MATTER
OF PRIDE

A
MATTER
OF PRIDE

by Emily Crofford

illustrated by Jim LaMarche

CAROLRHODA BOOKS, INC., MINNEAPOLIS

LIBRARY OF CONGRESS CATALOGING IN PUBLICATION DATA

Crofford, Emily.
A matter of pride.

SUMMARY: A young girl's opinion of her mother changes
as she watches the woman display her courage.

[1. Mothers and daughters—Fiction. 2. Courage—Fiction] I.
LaMarche, Jim. II. Title.

PZ7.C873Mat	[Fic]	81-3875
ISBN 0-87614-171-8		AACR2

1 2 3 4 5 6 7 8 9 10 86 85 84 83 82 81

to my brother Bill

Mother told Bill and me to be brave about going to the new school. But she wasn't brave about our new life on a cotton plantation in Arkansas.

I felt sorry for her, but I was ashamed of her too. She was afraid of everything. She warned us to watch out for snakes and said we were never to go near the big canal.

She said, "We're fortunate. Many families don't have homes. Many people don't have work." You could feel her sadness, though. And when the March wind blew down the pieces of newspaper pasted over the cracks in the walls, she cried.

Daddy wasn't afraid of anything. He had never plowed a mule before we moved, but he wasn't afraid of them. The mules belonged to the plantation owner. We didn't have any mules. Or pigs. Or a cow. We did have three chickens and a brown puppy that Bill had named Brownie. Bill, I told Mother, had no imagination. I would have named him Prince if I'd drawn the longest straw.

The thing Mother worried most about was not having a cow. "The children need milk," she said. "Especially Correy." Correy was Bill's and my little brother. He was going on three. "We'll sell the Victrola and buy a cow."

My mouth dropped open. We'd had to sell almost everything to pay for the move to Arkansas, but Mother had refused to part with the Victrola. Bill and I liked it too. Cranking it up and playing records was more fun than almost anything.

"That's not fair!" I was about to say, but Daddy was looking at me. I swallowed. "That's a good idea," I said.

"Let's have a good-bye party for the Victrola," Daddy said.

I put on "Broadway Melody," my favorite. Correy began to dance in circles, and Daddy bowed to Mother. "May I have this dance?" he asked.

"Why, thank you." Mother smiled up at him. She looked smaller than ever when she danced with Daddy. She reminded me of the china tea set I had gotten two Christmases ago, before Daddy had lost his job in Memphis.

"Well, come on," I said to Bill. "Let's dance before the Victrola runs down."

As it turned out, we didn't sell the Victrola after all. Nobody could afford to buy it. Instead, we all did things to save money. Daddy and Mother stopped drinking coffee. They dug up sassafras roots to make tea and picked poke salad and other wild greens to cook. Daddy gigged bullfrogs and caught fish in the canal. Bill and I picked dewberries on the ditch banks by our road. We caught crawfish and Mother cooked their tails.

Since it was spring when we moved, Bill and I didn't make many friends at school. Mostly we knew the kids we walked home with. Bill made friends with Timmy Bowers, also in third grade, and I tried to make friends with Grace Bowers, in fifth grade with me. It wasn't easy though. Grace was real moody, and besides, she and Timmy had to go straight home after school. Once when Timmy was dawdling, Grace had turned and yelled at him, "You better hurry up or Pa'll lay the razor strop across your back again." After that I stopped asking if they could stop and play. Grace never asked me to go to her house, but I couldn't have anyway because they lived on the other side of the canal, and Mother wouldn't let us cross the bridge.

On Saturdays, when Mr. Bowers went by in his wagon, I hoped he would bring Grace and Timmy and let them play awhile. But he never did. He never even waved back at me.

By the time the cotton came up and school

closed for summer, we had enough money to buy a cow. The day Daddy came leading her up the road, we all ran to meet them.

"It's my turn to name," I said.

"She already has a name," Daddy said. "Her name is Dolly."

"I think Violet is prettier," I said.

"Dolly's a pretty name," Mother said. "A pretty name for a perfectly gorgeous cow."

Dolly had nice eyes, big and brown and damp, but I certainly didn't think she was gorgeous. Her milk tasted delicious, though, especially with cornbread crumbled in it.

It was Bill's and Brownie's and my job to take Dolly to the plantation pasture every morning and bring her home in the evening. Daddy went with us a few times and taught Brownie to go into the pasture and circle Dolly until he separated her from the other cows. Then Brownie would herd her to the gate. When Bill and I began to go alone, Mother always warned us not to go into

the pasture ourselves. "And watch out for snakes and strange dogs," she would say.

When we were out of hearing, I'd answer, "Scaredy-cat, Mother."

We had just come back from the pasture one morning when Grace Bowers came into the yard.

"Grace!" I wanted to dance and sing. I hadn't had anybody but Bill to play with all summer.

Mother came out on the porch to welcome Grace. "I'll make some sugar biscuits," she said. "You all can have a tea party."

"Grace," I said pointedly, "crosses the bridge by herself."

"How old are you, Grace?" Mother asked.

"Twelve," Grace said.

"You're just ten, Meg. And since Grace has always lived here, I'm sure she isn't as curious and venturesome as you are."

That was a good example of her logic, I thought. I was too small to go exploring, but whenever I hid the scorched pans in the oven to get out

of washing them, she said I was too old for such nonsense.

I ignored Mother, and she went inside to make the sugar biscuits.

"What do you want to do, Grace?"

"Nothing." She glanced down the road. She had been doing that since she had come into the yard.

We sat down on the steps. "I'm closer to eleven," I said.

"You hear somebody coming?"

I shook my head, but she wasn't looking at me. "No, I don't hear anybody coming. I didn't know you were that old."

"I didn't start to school till I were—was nearly seven," Grace said. "And in second grade I got mumps and measles and whooping cough, so the teacher kept me back."

"You had all of them in one year?"

Grace nodded and after a minute said, "I won't be going to school at all after sixth grade."

I slapped at a fly that had settled on my arm but

missed. Grace didn't like for me to ask questions, but I couldn't help it. "You mean you're going to quit?"

"We all quit after sixth grade. My big brothers did and my sister did and I will too."

"School's not so bad," I said. "And you're really smart." Grace made a hundred on almost every test. And she often stayed inside at recess to read books Miss Connors brought from a library in town.

Grace looked at me the way she looked at her little brother when he said something especially dumb. Then she laughed. It was the first time I'd ever heard her laugh.

" 'School's not so bad,' " she mimicked me. "That's funny. That is really funny." She started laughing again, the way somebody laughs and cries at the same time when you tickle them too long. It made me uncomfortable. If Grace was going to be in one of her strange moods, I'd as soon she leave.

The awful laughing suddenly stopped. Grace

jumped up and scooted under the house.

I looked between the steps, but I couldn't see her. I wasn't sure whether I should crawl under and look for her or not.

"Are you playing a game?" I called.

I heard a muffled, "No." It sounded like Grace was crying. I got down on my hands and knees and went under.

The house sat three feet off the ground on cinder blocks so the water wouldn't get inside when the river rose and the ditches backed up. On hot days Bill and I played under there. I found Grace crouched behind one of the blocks with her face in her hands. She wasn't crying; she was shivering.

"Are you sick?"

Grace lifted her head and said in a low voice, "I'm supposed to be chopping corn. Pa's wagon's coming up the road."

"I didn't see it."

"I heard it coming across the bridge."

"Is he coming for you?" I was frightened now. I remembered the day Grace had told Timmy to hurry or their father would whip him with a razor strop.

"He don't know I'm here," Grace whispered. "He thinks I'm in the cornfield. Don't make a sound."

I sat close to Grace, hunched over to make myself small. The wagon went past and still Grace sat there shaking. Finally I crawled to the front of the house.

"I can't see the wagon," I said.

"Go out on the road and see if he's turned the corner."

I went to the footbridge and peered up the road. There was no sign of the wagon.

"You're safe," I called. "We can play now."

But Grace just scurried out from under the house like a frightened rabbit and, without a good-bye, ran toward her house.

For two weeks I kept hoping Grace would come back. I didn't ask to go see her. Mr. Bowers

might be there. Besides, I had figured out that Mother wouldn't let me or Bill go to the Bowers' house even if there wasn't a bridge.

The days, and the nights, grew hotter and hotter. We kept the milk and butter in the pump box to keep them from spoiling. The water we pumped from an underground spring made the box around the pump pipe damp and chill.

At night, until the air cooled enough to sleep, we sat on the front porch singing and watching heat lightning play in the thunderheads stacked on the horizon. One evening Daddy said, "It's not heat lightning this time. We're going to get rain."

We slept comfortably that night with the rain thumping on the roof. It hadn't slacked much when we awoke the next morning, and it kept on raining all week.

The rain wet the ground so deep that Daddy couldn't work even after it stopped. He spent the days at home. Bill and I could hear him and Mother talking sometimes in low voices.

They were worrying about his not getting paid for the days off and going deeper in debt at the plantation store.

On top of that Bill got sick with a fever and couldn't play outside. Summer, I thought, is boring, boring, boring!

One day I was in the front yard fishing for a doodlebug with a broomstraw when Daddy came outside. "The road is about dry," he said. "Let's go blackberry picking, Meg. Just you and me."

I was so excited I wanted to leave right then. I was going somewhere with Daddy. Just the two of us! But Mother made me put on overalls and a long-sleeved shirt first. And a sunhat. And my shoes.

When we reached the canal bridge, Daddy took my hand and we walked across the middle between the gouges cut by wagon wheels. I looked down between the boards. The water was a long way down, and it looked so cool. How I'd love to be down there in it.

"I don't know why Mother is so afraid of this bridge," I said.

"It isn't just this bridge, honey—although this is a bad one. When we used to have a car, your mother turned pale when we drove across any bridge."

"Why?"

"I don't know why. She doesn't either."

Maybe, I thought, it was like my panic when Miss Connors called on me to read aloud. Miss Connors said she was proud of me for trying even when I stumbled over words I knew. I didn't know why that happened either because I read aloud fine at home.

We passed a shotgun house and two box houses like the one we lived in. Then I saw a two-story house.

"Is that the Bowers' house?" I asked, although I was sure it was.

"Yep," was all Daddy said.

Mr. Bowers was not a hired worker like Daddy.

He rented an acreage and owned his own mules and farming tools. But from the looks of the Bowers' house, they weren't as rich as I'd thought they were. The paint was peeling and broken windows were patched with tarpaper. Behind the house, though, I could see part of a chicken house, which my family didn't have, and the barn was much larger than ours. It had a hayloft too. There were pigs and cows and mules in the lot, and farm equipment in the back yard.

In the front yard there were four trees. There weren't any trees in our yard. A pecan tree had a tire swing hung from a bottom limb. I didn't see Grace or Timmy. A big girl was hanging clothes on the line, but she didn't look toward us.

"It's a big house," I said.

Daddy grunted.

"The barn has a hayloft."

"Yep."

I didn't say any more.

We passed some land Mr. Bowers was clearing,

went around a curve, came to the end of the road, and went into a thicket. Inside the thicket the air hung still and smothering hot. Picking blackberries wasn't as much fun as I'd thought it would be. Mosquitoes bit my face and neck. Sweat ran down into my eyes and blackberry briars scratched my hands.

Daddy said we had filled the bucket quickly, but to me it seemed like we were there for hours. When we finally left the thicket and stepped back onto the road, I sighed and said, "The breeze feels wonderful."

Daddy motioned for me to be quiet. "Listen."

I heard it too—a man's angry voice. Daddy broke into a long stride, and I had to trot to keep up with him. When we rounded the curve, I put my hand over my mouth to keep from screaming.

Mr. Bowers had hitched a mule to a stump to make him pull it out of the ground. The mule was straining so hard its muscles bulged. Yelling at the mule to pull harder, Mr. Bowers was hitting

it with a rope. Blood dripped down the mule's hip.

His face like a thundercloud, Daddy plunked down the bucket of berries. "Go home, Meg!"

Choking and sobbing, I ran. I was still crying and trying to get my breath when I got home. Mother mopped my face with a wet cloth. "Meg, what's wrong? Where is Daddy?"

"Mr. Bowers...his mule...whipping him. Daddy went..."

Mother's face turned white.

A moment later Daddy came in, the bucket of berries in one hand, the rope with blood on it in the other. Looking at Mother, he said, "I didn't touch him." He went to the kitchen stove, jerked open the firebox door, and shoved in the rope.

Several times I told Bill about how brave Daddy had been, how he had jumped the ditch to make Mr. Bowers stop beating the mule. But when school started, neither Grace nor I mentioned what had happened.

We'd been back in school for just two weeks

when Daddy came in one morning from going out to milk and set an empty bucket on the table.

"Dolly's gone," he said.

Mother, fixing oatmeal, stopped with the spoon in midair.

"She broke out of the lot."

Mother let out her breath and put the lid on the oatmeal.

"I thought you were going to say she'd been stolen. Maybe she just went off to the pasture by herself this morning."

"I've been to the pasture."

"Then she's probably grazing on the canal bank," Mother said cheerfully. "She'll come home when she needs milking bad enough."

"I hope so," Daddy said. "I don't have time to look—I have to go to work."

"We'll stay home from school and go look for her," I said.

"Oh, no you won't!"

I knew it was useless to argue. Daddy was as

bad as Mother about school. He came to the table and hugged me. "I'm proud of you for wanting to help, though," he said.

I thought that surely Mother would offer to look for Dolly when he said that. But she didn't. She kissed him good-bye and served the oatmeal— with yesterday's cream. I kept staring at her, thinking, You're afraid of the canal, coward!

Mother knew what I was thinking, all right. Her neck turned bright pink.

"I couldn't manage both Dolly and Correy if I did find her," she said.

"Sure," I mumbled and pushed my bowl away.

When Bill and I got home from school, Dolly hadn't come back.

"Meg and I'll go look," Bill said. "We'll take Brownie."

"All right," Mother said. "But be careful. Don't walk near the edge of the bridge."

I almost dropped my books. Mother had given us permission to go on the canal bridge!

After we had changed clothes, we went outside and explained to Brownie that we wanted him to help us find Dolly. He sniffed the road, jumped the ditch, and bounded through the field—chasing a rabbit.

"Come back here, you dummy!" I hollered. In books dogs can track anything. They don't even have to have it spelled out for them.

Brownie came back, wagging his tail like he thought we should congratulate him.

Bill said, "I'll get some of Dolly's hay for him to sniff. Then he'll understand."

Brownie sniffed the hay—and sneezed. Thoroughly disgusted with him, I scolded, "And we thought you were smart."

"He is," Bill said, and glared at me, then kicked a clod of dirt so hard it made a dust shower.

From the middle of the bridge we looked up and down the canal banks. We could see bushes and patches of grass, but no cows. Bill and Brownie went across. Ignoring Bill's reminder that Mother said not to do it, I ambled to the edge. There was no railing, but that didn't scare me. Nobody could accuse *me* of being chicken. I peered down. Far below, fast water foamed around sharp rocks. It made me dizzy; I felt like I was going to fall. Holding my breath, I inched backward to the middle, then ran to the bank. When I could trust my voice to work, I said, "Dolly could be in the thicket where Daddy and I went blackberry picking."

As we neared the Bowers' house, I told Bill, "There it is. That's where Grace and Timmy live."

"Uh-huh."

That aggravated me. Bill never got excited about anything.

I didn't see anybody in the Bowers' yard. Mr. Bowers was a speck at the other end of the field. "I wonder why the kids stop going to school when they get through sixth grade."

"Because Mr. Bowers makes them," Bill said.

"That's as high as he went."

I stopped walking and stared at him. "That doesn't make any sense."

Bill shrugged. "That's what Timmy told me."

I was going to ask him to repeat exactly what Timmy had said, but Brownie leaped across the roadside ditch. Bill and I tried to jump it too, but we landed in the mud. We got ourselves unstuck and ran through the field behind Brownie. This time, I knew, he was not chasing a rabbit. He was acting just the way he did when he went into the pasture to bring Dolly out.

Dolly was tied to the Bowers' chicken house with a heavy rope. We were wondering what to do when an ugly, white pit dog came from the barn. His eyes were squinty and mean-looking; his teeth looked like they could bite your hand off. Brownie bristled and the pit dog growled. Neither of them could back down. Brownie had to protect us, and this was the pit dog's yard.

The thought that they might fight made my

stomach curl up, and Bill looked like he had stopped breathing.

We did what Daddy had taught us to do if Brownie was about to get into a fight: without a word we turned and walked slowly away. Brownie followed us. The pit dog went back to the barn.

We ran all the way home. "We found Dolly!" I told Mother.

Bill said, "Mr. Bowers has her tied up. Brownie found her."

As if she thought she hadn't heard right, Mother repeated, "Mr. Bowers—has her tied up?"

Bill nodded. "To the chicken house. Brownie and his pit dog almost got into a fight."

"Daddy will go for her when he gets home," I said.

Mother gazed over the top of my head. I knew she was thinking about what might happen if Daddy went for Dolly.

"No," Mother said. "We'll go for her."

"You'll have to cross the bridge," I said.

She was whetting the rabbit-skinning knife and didn't answer.

"We'll have to jump the ditch. You'll get your shoes muddy."

She dropped the knife into her pocketbook. "Go lock Brownie in the barn, Bill." She put shoes on Correy. "Let's go," she said.

As we walked, I kept looking at Mother. I'd never seen her like this before. At the bridge her face turned pale, but with her eyes straight ahead and her jaw so tight it looked like it might break, she marched across.

She didn't cut across the field to the chicken house. She went right up the Bowers' front path. At the bottom of the steps, she said, "Stay here," and went up to the door, paying no attention to the pit dog snuffling at her heels. I could hear a baby crying inside and children yelling at each other. I looked around for Mr. Bowers. He was weighing cotton at the other end of the field.

Except for the baby crying, the noise stopped

when Mother knocked. Mrs. Bowers opened the door. She rubbed her dress, trying to smooth out the wrinkles.

"It's yore cow, ain't it?" she said. "I—I'm sorry."

"I'm sorry she got out," Mother said. "I'm going to take her home now."

Mrs. Bowers only nodded and closed the door.

At the chicken house, Mother told me to take care of Correy and handed Bill her pocketbook. She tried to untie the knots in the rope but couldn't. Mr. Bowers had tied them hard and Dolly had pulled them tighter. Mother took out the knife and started sawing at the rope, halfway between Dolly's nose and the chicken house.

I had stopped watching Mother. Mr. Bowers was coming toward his house. He had seen us. I sucked in my breath. "He's coming," I said. "Mother, he's coming."

Mr. Bowers didn't run, didn't even seem to be in a hurry. He took long, deliberate steps, bearing down on us. I pulled Correy close to me. Bill put the pocketbook between his feet and clenched his fists.

Mother didn't glance up.

Mr. Bowers didn't speak until he was within three feet of us. "Leave her be. It's yore husband I want to come for her."

Mother kept sawing at the rope. "She needs milking," she said. Her voice was calm, but her fingers were shaking.

I felt shivery, but I was sweating the way I had in the thicket. I'd never seen Mr. Bowers up close. His shoulders were hunched and some of his fingers were crippled, but it was his eyes that made my heart pound. They were hard, and mean.

"Leave her be," he said again. "A man what can't master his stock ought not to have any. Ought not to be here in the first place. His kind ain't wanted."

The last cord snapped, and Mother handed the knife to Bill and started to lead Dolly away.

"She better not ever come on my land again," Mr. Bowers said.

Mother looked straight up into his eyes and said quietly, "If she should, please send word and we'll come immediately. Good afternoon, Mr. Bowers."

Correy wanted to be with Bill, so I took Mother's pocketbook. Dolly moved slowly because her full udder hurt, and Bill and Correy got ahead of us.

"Poor Dolly," Mother said to her. "I'll milk you as soon as we get home."

"Mr. Bowers is a terrible man," I said.

"Don't be too hard on him, Meg. I suppose his pride makes him that way."

I didn't understand his kind of pride. He looked like it made even him miserable. Mine made me happy. I was so proud of Mother I wanted to do cartwheels. She might be afraid of snakes, and bridges, and Mr. Bowers, but she was not a coward. As Miss Connors said, you had to be especially brave to do things that frightened you.

Just before we reached the bridge I took my mother's free hand and held it until we were home.